First published 1996 by Methuen
an imprint of Reed Children's Books
Michelin House, 81 Fulham Road, London SW3 6RB
and Auckland, Melbourne, Singapore and Toronto.

ISBN 1 85591 546 4

Printed in Italy

Hunnypot Library

Winnie-the-Pooh
Builds a House for Eeyore

From the Stories by A.A. Milne

With new and adapted illustrations
in the style of E.H. Shepard

METHUEN

One day Pooh Bear went round
to Piglet's house to see what Piglet
was doing. It was snowing and he
expected to find Piglet warming
his toes in front of his fire. To Pooh's
surprise the door was open, and
Piglet wasn't there.

"He's out," said Pooh sadly. "I
shall have to go on a fast thinking
walk by myself. Bother!"

But first he thought that he would
knock very loudly just to make *quite*
sure. While he waited a hum came
into his head, which seemed to him
a Good Hum.

The more it snows
(Tiddely pom),
The more it goes
(Tiddely pom),
The more it goes
(Tiddely pom),
On snowing.
And nobody knows
(Tiddely pom),
How cold my toes
(Tiddely pom),
How cold my toes
(Tiddely pom),
Are growing.

Pooh decided to go home to see what time it was before going to visit Eeyore and sing his song to him.

His mind was so busy with the hum that, when he got home and suddenly saw Piglet sitting in his best arm-chair, he could only stand there wondering whose house he was in.

"Hallo, Piglet," he said.

He looked up at his clock, which had stopped at five minutes to eleven some weeks ago.

"Nearly eleven o'clock," said Pooh happily. "You're just in time for a little smackerel of something. And then we'll go out, Piglet, and sing my song to Eeyore."

"Which song, Pooh?"

"The one we're going to sing to Eeyore," explained Pooh.

Half an hour later they set out on their way. The snow fluttered around. Piglet was feeling more snowy behind the ears than he had ever felt before.

"Pooh," he said a little timidly, because he didn't want Pooh to think he was giving in, "how would it be if we went home and *practised* your song, and then sang it to Eeyore tomorrow?"

"That's a very good idea, Piglet," said Pooh. "We'll practise it now as we go along. But it's no good going home to practise it, because it's a special Outdoor Song which Has To Be Sung In The Snow."

"Are you sure?" asked Piglet anxiously.

"Well, you'll see, Piglet, because this is how it begins. *The more it snows, tiddely pom –*"

"Tiddely what?" said Piglet.

"Pom," said Pooh. "*The more it goes, tiddely pom, the more —*"

"Didn't you say snows?"

"Yes, but that was *before*."

"Before the tiddely pom?"

"It was a *different* tiddely pom," said Pooh, feeling rather muddled. "I'll sing it to you properly and then you'll see." So he sang it again.

By this time they were getting
near Eeyore's Gloomy Place. It was
still very snowy so they turned into a
little pine-wood, and sat down on
the gate which led into it. To keep
themselves warm they sang Pooh's
song right through six times, Piglet
doing the tiddely-poms and Pooh
doing the rest of it. In a little while
they felt much warmer, and were
able to talk again.

"I've been thinking about Eeyore,"
said Pooh. "Poor Eeyore has nowhere
to live. We all have houses but poor
Eeyore has nothing. So let's build
him a house."

"Where shall we build it?" asked Piglet.

"We will build it here," said Pooh, "by this wood, out of the wind, because this is where I thought of it. We will call this Pooh Corner. And we will build an Eeyore House with sticks for Eeyore."

"There was a heap of sticks on the other side of the wood," said Piglet.

"Thank you, Piglet," said Pooh, and off they went to fetch the sticks.

Christopher Robin had spent the morning indoors and was just wondering what it was like outside, when Eeyore knocked on the door.

"How are you, Eeyore?" said Christopher Robin.

"It's snowing still," said Eeyore gloomily. "*And* freezing. However," he said, brightening up a little, "we haven't had an earthquake lately."

"What's the matter, Eeyore?"

"Nothing, Christopher Robin. Nothing important. I suppose you haven't seen a house anywhere about?"

"Who lives there?"

"I do. At least I thought I did. After all, we can't all have houses."

"But Eeyore, I didn't know –"

"I don't know how it is, Christopher Robin," Eeyore interrupted, "but what with all this snow and one thing and another it isn't so Hot in my field about three o'clock in the morning. Quite-between-ourselves-and-don't-tell-anybody, it's Cold."

"Oh, Eeyore!"

"And I said to myself: The others will be sorry if I'm getting myself all cold."

"Oh, Eeyore!" said Christopher Robin, feeling very sorry already.

"So what it all comes to is that I built myself a house down by my little wood."

"How exciting!"

"The really exciting part," said Eeyore sadly, "is that when I left it this morning it was there, and when I came back it wasn't."

"We'll go and look for it at once," Christopher Robin said to Eeyore, and off they hurried.

Soon they got to where Eeyore's house wasn't any longer.

"There!" said Eeyore. "Not a stick of it left!"

But Christopher Robin wasn't listening to Eeyore, he was listening to something else.

"Can you hear it?" he asked.

They both listened...and they heard a deep gruff voice saying in a singing voice that the more it snowed the more it went on snowing, and a small high voice tiddely-pomming in between.

"It's Pooh," said Christopher Robin excitedly..."*And* Piglet!"

"Probably," said Eeyore.

The words of the song changed suddenly.

"*We've finished our HOUSE!*" sang the gruff voice.

"*Tiddely pom!*" sang the squeaky one.

"Pooh!" shouted Christopher Robin...

The singers stopped suddenly.

"It's Christopher Robin!" said Pooh eagerly.

"He's round by the place where we got all those sticks from," said Piglet.

They hurried round the corner of the wood.

"Why, here *is* Eeyore," said Pooh, when he had finished hugging Christopher Robin, and he nudged Piglet and they thought to themselves what a lovely surprise they had got ready. "Hallo, Eeyore."

"Same to you, Pooh Bear, and twice on Thursdays," said Eeyore gloomily.

Before Pooh could say: "Why Thursdays?" Christopher Robin began to explain the sad story of Eeyore's Lost House. And Pooh and Piglet listened, and their eyes seemed to get bigger and bigger.

"*Where* did you say it was?" asked Pooh.

"Just here," said Eeyore.

"Made of sticks?"

"Yes."

"Oh!" said Piglet.

"What?" said Eeyore.

"I just said 'Oh!'" said Piglet nervously.

"You're sure it *was* a house?" said Pooh. "And you're sure it was here?"

"Of course I am," said Eeyore.

"Why, what's the matter, Pooh?" asked Christopher Robin.

"Well," said Pooh…"The fact *is*," said Pooh…"It's like this," said Pooh, and something seemed to tell him that he wasn't explaining very well, and he nudged Piglet again.

"It's like this," said Piglet quickly… "Only warmer," he added after deep thought.

"What's warmer?"

"The other side of the wood, where Eeyore's house is."

"My house?" said Eeyore.

"My house was here."

"No," said Piglet firmly. "The other side of the wood."

"Because of being warmer," said Pooh.

They came round the corner, and there was Eeyore's house, looking as comfy as anything.

"There you are," said Piglet.

Eeyore went inside...and came out again.

"It's a remarkable thing," he said. "It *is* my house, so the wind must have blown it here. Here it is as good as ever. In fact, better in places."

"Much better," said Pooh and Piglet together.

"It just shows what can be done by taking a little trouble," said Eeyore. "Do you see? Brains first and then Hard Work. T*hat's* the way to build a house," said Eeyore proudly.

So they left him in it; and Christopher Robin went back to lunch with his friends Pooh and Piglet, and on the way they told him of the Awful Mistake they had made. When he had finished laughing, they all sang the Outdoor Song for Snowy Weather the rest of the way home, with Piglet putting in the tiddely-poms again.